P   Fred's first day

Warren, Cathy

p90-37

DATE DUE		
NOV 27 1990		
JUL 16 1991		
JUL 22 1991		
APR 19 1994		
MAY 16 1994		
OCT 31 1997		
NOV 30 1998		
JAN 11 1999		

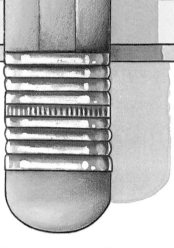

For Mom and Dad,

who made my place in the middle

fit just right—C.W.

For Chuku—P. C.

Text copyright © 1984 by Cathy Warren
Illustrations copyright © 1984 by Pat Cummings
First Edition   1 2 3 4 5 6 7 8 9 10

Library of Congress Cataloging in Publication Data
Warren, Cathy.   Fred's first day.
   Summary: After a few false starts, Fred's first day at nursery school turns out to be just right.
   [1. Nursery schools—Fiction. 2. Afro-Americans—Fiction. 3. Schools—Fiction]
I. Cummings, Pat, ill. II. Title. PZ7.W2514Fr 1984   [E]   83-25153
ISBN 0-688-03813-1   ISBN 0-688-03814-X (lib. bdg.)

Fred's First Day

by Cathy Warren

pictures by Pat Cummings

Lothrop, Lee & Shepard Books
New York

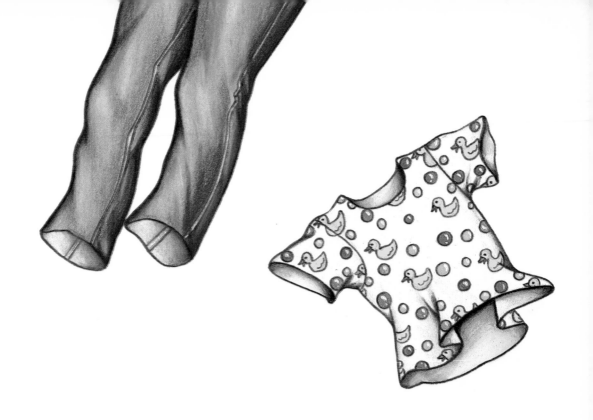

There are three children in Fred's family.

There is Sam, Baby Bob, and Fred in the middle.

Fred's not quite big enough to wear Sam's clothes.

But he's much too big for Baby Bob's.

Nothing seems to fit him just right.

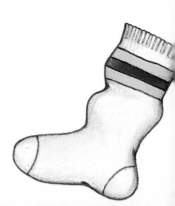

Fred loves to climb trees with Sam.

But Sam's tree house is much too high.

Fred tries to climb all the way to the top.

But sometimes he falls.

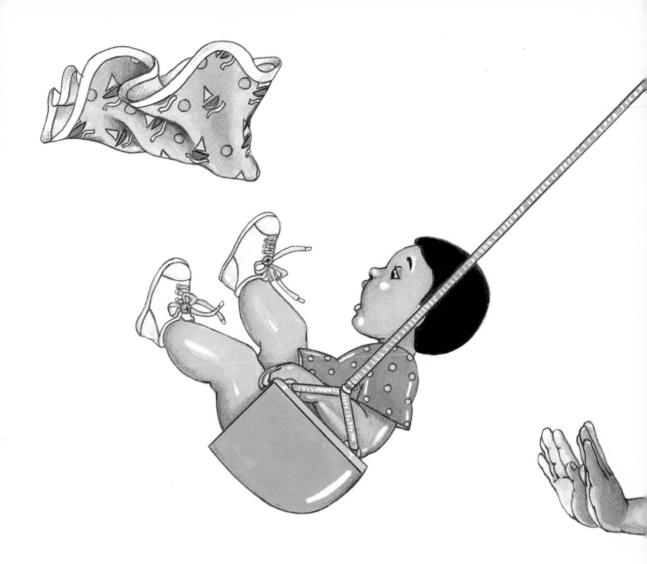

"Careful," his mother warns.

He has bandages all over himself.

He loves to swing Baby Bob and hug him too.

But sometimes he pushes too fast and hugs too hard.

"Gentle," his mother reminds him.

One morning not so long ago,

Fred tried to build a model airplane with Sam.

But he had to be so careful!

"Too rough," cried Sam. "Out of my room."

"You're not big enough," his mother explained.

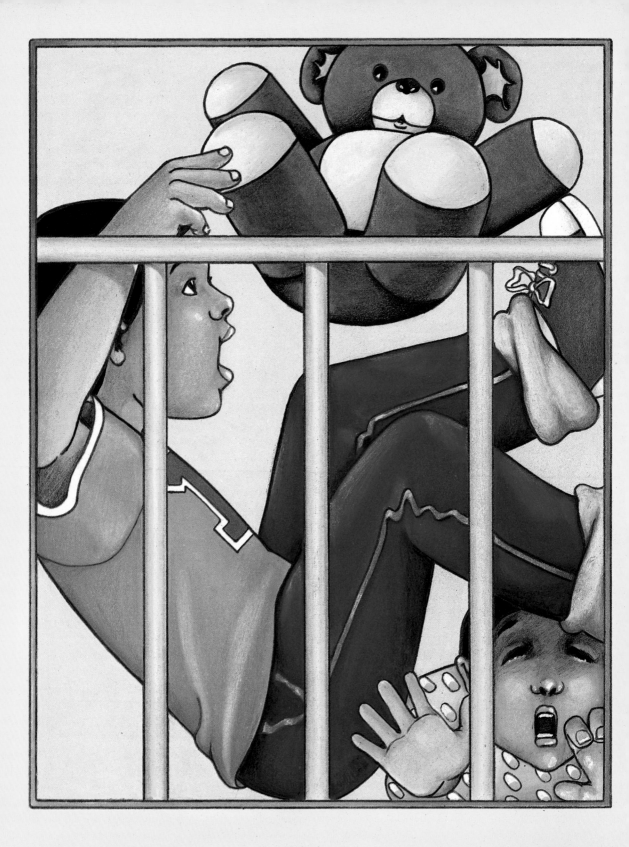

Then he tried playing with Baby Bob.

He climbed into the playpen with him.

But he had to be so gentle!

"Hurt," yelled Baby Bob.

"You're too big," his mother told him.

"I will find a place just for you," she said.

And she did.

It was the Sunshine School, down the street.

"Tomorrow will be your first day," she told Fred.

"I'm just sure you're going to love it."

Fred wasn't so sure.

That afternoon, he sat in the backyard

beneath his favorite tree.

He wondered about his new school.

Would all the children be big like Sam

or little like Baby Bob?

Would his new teacher be nice?

When he finally went inside, it was dark and time for bed.

In the morning, his mother dressed him in a new shirt

and put a fresh bandage in his pocket.

Before she left Fred at the school,

she gave him a kiss on his broad little head.

"I see boys and girls your size," she said.

They were sitting in a circle on the floor.

The teacher seemed nice.

She smiled and said, "Welcome, Fred. Come join us."

Fred sat down.

But he forgot to be gentle.

He scrunched little Wanda's hand.

"Yeow," she screamed.

Then she began to cry.

She cried during most of story time.

And she cried in line behind Fred during painting too.

At free time, Fred forgot to be careful.

He knocked down the tall tower the other boys had built.

"He's too rough," they said to one another.

"We don't want to play with him."

All during snack, nobody sat next to Fred but Wanda.

And she was still crying.

Fred felt sad and lonesome, and he just wanted to go home.

Some of the other children were ready to go home too.

They started looking out the windows for their parents.

When the teacher noticed, she cried, "Playtime!"

"Hurrah," they all shouted.

They hurried onto the playground.

Fred took a turn on the swings.

He climbed easily into the low tree house

where the other boys were playing.

Suddenly, the boy next to him yelled, "Watch me.

I'm an airplane."

He jumped out of the tree house.

But he didn't fly.

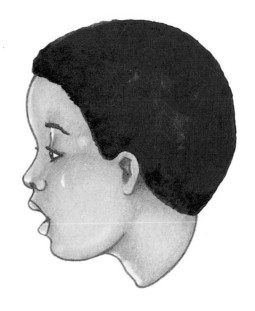

Instead, he landed on the ground and skinned his knee.

He began to cry.

Wanda joined in.

"I want my mommy," she wailed.

"There, there," said the teacher.

Fred felt sorry for the boy.

And he felt sorry for Wanda too.

He took the bandage from his pocket and put it

on the boy's knee, ever so carefully.

Then he hugged Wanda, ever so gently.

The boy stopped crying.

So did Wanda.

When they went back inside, Wanda held Fred's hand.

The boys began to play with Fred.

They helped him build a tall tower.

Even Wanda pitched in.

They were so busy, they didn't notice their parents

looking in the windows.

Fred was the last to leave.

Baby Bob wanted to stay and play.

"You're not big enough," his mother said.

"But someday, this school will fit you like it fits me—
just right," Fred told him.

He gave Baby Bob a kiss on his broad little head.

And they walked on home,

with Fred in the middle.